Even
More
Parts

Even More Parts

IDIOMS FROM HEAD TO TOE

Quit messing with my head!

Tedd Arnold

Dial Books for Young Readers New York

To Walter —
For the part you played

Published by Dial Books for Young Readers
A division of Penguin Young Readers Group
345 Hudson Street
New York, New York 10014

Typography by Nancy R. Leo-Kelly
Manufactured in China on acid-free paper
1 3 5 7 9 10 8 6 4 2

Library of Congress Cataloging-in-Publication Data
Arnold, Tedd.
Even more parts : idioms from head to toe / Tedd Arnold.
p.   cm.
Summary: A young boy is worried about what will happen to his body when
he hears such expressions as "I'm tongue-tied," "Don't give me any of your lip,"
and "I put my foot in my mouth."
ISBN 0-8037-2938-3
[1. Body, Human—Fiction. 2. Figures of speech—Fiction.
3. Stories in rhyme.] I. Title.
PZ8.3.A647Ev 2004   [E]—dc22   2003056170

The art was prepared using color pencils and watercolor washes,
and the text was hand-lettered by the artist.

Sometimes I wish my stupid ears
Weren't always open wide.
They hear such strange and crazy talk—
I'm scared to go outside!

I jotted down a list of all
The scary things I've heard.
Believe me, all of these are real.
I wrote them word for word.

To leave my bedroom unprepared,
I'd have to be a fool!
Excuse me now. There's work to do
Before I go to school.

There are so many **crazy** things
I have to keep in mind!
I sure don't want to accidentally
Leave my parts behind.

Mom says, "Dear, it's time for school.
Let's go or you'll be late."
Then Dad says, "Just remember, son...

"Keep your head on straight!"